URSAMER

Treasury Of Feel-Good Stories Book 2

KARINA MCROBERTS

ALSO BY KARINA MCROBERTS

The Palace of the Stars

The Mine's Eye

The Light

Galla of Chelandra – Healer Mage

Master of the World – Love and Courage

Juggernaut – Evil and Justice

A Man for All Seasons (audio)

Dargo – Eco Hero

The Haunting of York

The Girl With Ten Diamonds

Charlie's Ark

Welcome to My Sketchbook

Creative Writing for Beginners

This book is dedicated to Ira Nugapigak.
I remember.

ACKNOWLEDGMENTS

My heartfelt thanks to my wonderful supporters: Bill McRoberts, Nicola Smith, Elizabeth K. Dennis, Boyko Ovcharov, and everyone at Next Chapter. Also, I salute these fabulous image artists: Lufimorgan, Ion Don, Jimmy More, Jacz, Nejron, Pongsuwan, Jin Filim, Canopus, Yuran78, Sin Jin, Wacomka, Belchonock, and Plancton.

Heart of Gold
Body of Iron
Mind of Steel
Spirit of Light

CONTENTS

CHAPTER 1
WRONG PLACE, RIGHT TIME

THE GIRL APPEARED. She just appeared! Certainly she wasn't there just one moment ago.

She appeared to the lady who was homeless.

But, this was the lady's bench. Her tiny little piece of the park. So, homeless she was not. Not quite.

She was hot and wished the breeze would pick up. Instead of a breeze, a small child had blown in. A strange looking little girl, even by New York standards.

And dressed for winter! How could she stand it? But the child did not seem to mind.

The lady sat up on her bench. It was getting harder to do without help. But she managed, and felt a small tickle of pride at that. Small things matter a lot when you have no home. Counting your meager blessings becomes an art form.

"Hello, dear elder," the child remarked. She didn't say more, not at first. Her people took their time about most things.

"Hello to you," the old woman of the park bench replied with a smile in her voice. Children seldom stopped to speak with her and often tormented her. But this girl looked different. And, she smiled back.

It was only then that the homeless woman noticed the child had a sled, of all things! Central Park was great for sleds, but not in summer. And, upon that sled were a puppy and a huge chunk of ice, which was not doing at all well under the circumstance of a muggy August day. She decided not to allude to these things and asked the little girl's name.

"My name is Uŕsamer."

Here was a lovely girl of perhaps eight or nine with deep brown eyes and a radiant smile. The old woman wondered where she'd come from. There were all kinds of people in New York, of course, but not so many like this girl.

And her clothes were strange! Yes, that was it! Eskimo clothes! Rather, Inuit.

How odd, the woman thought. *It's hotter than hell's handrails today.*

She replied, "That's a pretty name. Mine's Granny. Well, not really, but everyone calls me that."

Uŕsamer struggled with the little English she knew. But managed, "I greet you, kindly Grandmother. My dog, Nuga. Is there any food he could eat? Nuga grows and grows. Nuga always hungry. Is there somewhere I fish for him?"

No one in their right mind would eat any fish that came out of the East River, Central Park Pond, or anywhere else around here. But as luck would have it, Granny had just finished her morning rummage and had scrounged some trashed burger bits.

The child smiled. Her dog hopped down off the sled and gobbled up the food.

Uŕsamer moved closer to Granny's face, intending to rub noses, but the woman backed away.

Not so long after the first Covid tsunami, she thought. *What a horrible time that was. Nature sure is angry with us.*

The lady had survived by grabbing all the edible rubbish she could and crawling into an unused subway tunnel. It was tough down there, and she couldn't wait to get back up to the surface. But that was another story, and Granny didn't wish to burden the child with it.

Uŕsamer did not approach further, but her face showed confusion. And hurt. Luckily, the puppy clambered up to Granny and licked her face in thanks. Nuga had very good manners. And that broke the ice, so to speak. Now, Uŕsamer regarded the block of ice she carried on her sled. "Ice melting, kindly Grandmother! Bears in sea!"

"Eh? Oh yes, dear, I know. Where do you come from, by the way? Aren't you hot in those furs? And, aren't *you* hungry?"

"No, I fine, thank you. But need find great place where make great changes. Ice *melting*, Grandmother!"

"Great place? Great changes?" *What's this little girl so desperate about?*

"Hmm, perhaps you mean the United Nations?"

"Is great place?"

"Well, yes, I suppose so."

"How we get there?"

"Well, it's a bit of a hike, dear. How did *you* get here, anyway?"

Ursamer was about to answer when two big men, dressed alike in dark blue, began walking towards them.

Ursamer drained some ice into a cup and offered it to the woman on the bench. "Here, Grandmother. Thank you for good help."

Ursamer's dog growled as the men in blue came closer. He was pretty sure they would not understand.

Ursamer, Nuga, sled, ice – all faded fast, white into the hot air.

* * *

"Hey Eddie, look at this," the chief officer remarked.

"Looks like sled tracks, Sarge. Weird. Who'd bring a sled out here in the middle of summer?"

"Probl'y some nut," Sarge replied. We get all kinds of 'em, don't we?"

Eddie winked knowingly at Granny as his boss began to move off.

When his partner wasn't looking, Eddie slipped Granny a donut. Granny gave the rookie cop her very best smile. She knew her gift was equally important.

CHAPTER 2
DESPERATION

THE NEXT PLACE in which Uŕsamer found herself was not a happy one. Like the last one, there were a lot of people. She had never seen so many, many people! Why were they all here?

She asked about any great places where great changes were to be made, but no one seemed to know. When she asked about the Unity of Nations, their eyes lit up. They all began pushing and shoving each other, holding out their hands, beseeching.

She was going to ask for food for Nuga, but it was soon apparent to her that these tall, dark, angry people had nothing to spare.

They came towards Uŕsamer and Nuga. She had never seen people like this before.

Uŕsamer knew this was no place for her. She would have to look elsewhere!

Her language skills were limited. No one spoke Inuit! She knew a little English from school, but not very much. And besides, these angry rants didn't sound anything like English.

This is why she had started out with the biggest ice block she could carry. No words would be needed. She showed it to the angry people, but they did not understand. What they did seem to understand was the nutritional value of Nuga! They looked at him with eyes turned to stones. Stones of hot fire. Nuga barked and growled.

Uŕsamer knew this was not the right place, and

no place for them indeed. They had to go somewhere different. Some place colder.

A man reached out and grabbed Uŕsamer's pup. Nuga bit him. The man yelped and let go. Taking some of her last dried fish and tossing it to the man—girl, dog, and ice, sledded fast away into the ether.

* * *

Uŕsamer found she had no control over where they travelled. Or in what season they travelled.

Why, she didn't know. Otherwise, she believed her plan was good.

But now she felt utterly despondent. Things weren't working out as she'd hoped. People didn't seem to understand about the ice. But she had to *make* them understand!

She had to get to a place where they'd be safer, and somewhere where she could get more food for Nuga. And, although Uŕsamer had started out with the biggest block of ice she could carry, she had to get to a place where the ice might last a bit longer. And, most importantly, somewhere where people would *listen!*

CHAPTER 3
EARLESS

THIS ALSO, was a busy, noisy place. The noise nearly drove her mad; she who was accustomed to hearing wind and sea, bears, seals, and birds.

Uŕsamer and Nuga found themselves in a shopping mall! It was tolerably cool here. And here it was winter. That was certainly an improvement.

But the noise! All the people! Again, great mobs of them, hurrying every which way.

Uŕsamer decided to just watch and wait. Wait for an intelligent person who would listen. She sat down on a bench and thought she might have to wait there for an eternity.

A woman pointed at them and said, "Oh, will look at that? What a cute little girl! And that puppy!"

A man remarked, "She must be a Christmas display. Look, she has a sled."

Uŕsamer and Nuga sat very still. She knew right away these were not the right people.

"Oh! She's *real!* Hello. Are you a Christmas display?"

Uŕsamer was tired and she did not understand what the shopping woman was saying to her, so she said nothing in return and pointed to the ice.

But the woman and the shopping man with her did not comprehend.

The man remarked, "Well, at least you could *say* something. You're very rude, you know that?"

"She's no good, Daddy. What a stupid display. Let's go see the Elf Bots. They're *real.*" The boy pulled an ugly face at Uŕsamer and walked away, urging his parents along behind him.

Uŕsamer and Nuga sat for a very long time. They were both tired and disheartened. They rested until another woman, this one in uniform, approached them. She bent down to look Uŕsamer in the eye.

"Why, hello there. And what's your name?"

Nuga had set up a low growl, so Uŕsamer responded cautiously—no smile this time. "My name is Uŕsamer."

"Yes. I heard you were here. You've been here

for quite a while. Where are your parents? Are you lost?"

Ursamer knew enough English to realize what the woman as asking, and she did not want to talk to her about her family. A huge tear welled up in one eye, and then the other. Soon many silent tears were falling, followed by more. Nuga whined and snuggled up to her.

The woman remarked, "Well, this won't do now, will it? Come along, I'll take you to my office, and then we can get down to business. A child abandoned. No excuse for it nowadays. Plenty of tracking apps. My goodness, and where have you been? Dressed like that? And you're *dirty*. Filthy! And that dog! Where'd you get him? Off the street? He's so scrawny. And he stinks like fish. Yuk! You can't have dogs in here!"

Ursamer could not understand all the words, but she knew this woman was no listener, she never drew breath; and was, therefore, of absolutely no use whatsoever.

The woman grabbed hold of Ursamer's hand. Nuga growled and snapped at her. The woman hit Nuga with a big black stick. He yelped and let go, but latched onto Ursamer's cloak, trying to pull the child away from the stick woman.

The woman chained Ursamer to the bench, Nuga still attached.

"Damned animal! I saw him stealing food off that cart. Don't think I didn't! He might even be rabid! Ever thought of that? He'll have to be put down, and I suspect you'll be off to child services, so you'd best calm down and behave yourself."

The mall cop turned to grab her radio. When she turned back, an empty pair of cuffs swung from the bench.

But there were tracks; a set of parallel tracks marring the highly polished floor. Ending abruptly, they led nowhere.

CHAPTER 4
THE ONE THING

TWO CHILDREN STOOD in the courtyard of a small hotel that had placed itself within a section of what *was* a forest, now gone. A red-haired boy of about eleven years, and a small Inuit girl. This mesmerizing creature, dressed traditionally in furs and mukluk boots, was nine years old, and the boy had been very curious about her ever since she'd appeared at what was left of his parents' hotel. That was it, just appeared. From nowhere whatsoever.

Strange as it seemed, she looked to be on her own—and how could that be, he wondered? Bailey, for that was the boy's name, had been working up courage to speak to her. But she beat him to it.

"My name is Uŕsamer."

"What kind of a name is that?"

It just came out; for some reason she made him nervous. He'd not meant to offend. But before he could try again, the girl replied, "I am called after the great sea bears."

Ursamer was pretty sure the boy could not understand her. Just like the others. But she knew, this one had to understand. Because he was the right one. This one would listen with his heart. And because of this, no matter what language she employed, he would be able understand.

She retrieved something from a pocket in her parka and placed it into the boy's hand. At first he was afraid; but he was also awestruck, so he kept his hand out.

Magic glowed in Bailey's hand. It looked like ice, but carried fire within. It looked like nothing he had ever seen! Finely beautiful...like a *star*. And that indeed was what it was.

Then Ursamer laid her hand upon the glowing thing. Now, when she spoke in her own language, Bailey could understand her every word.

"Sea bear?" he queried. "Oh, you mean a polar bear."

"Yes." She said nothing more, but stared off into some private distant reality. Bailey remained perplexed but absolutely fascinated.

And then, still staring, she intoned, "The bears are in the sea now. This is not right. They will tire and drown."

The boy didn't know how to respond; kicked the sand, trying not to be awkward. "Whaddya doing here?"

"Well, right now I am speaking with you." She smiled, and this made him feel infinitely better. More at ease.

Another kind of ice was breaking, and this encouraged Ursamer. She found she could speak much more eloquently than ever before. She was delighted, and so continued, "But *just* now, I was standing on the deck, the one above us, looking down onto a sea of diamonds. A canopy of jewels. The sunlight spicing the windy rain with glittering tree stars.

"Everything swayed. The wind swayed, the rain swayed, the trees swayed. It was like a dance.

"Then a great gust blew through and shattered all the crystals. It was magnificent! Did you see it?"

"How could you see *that*? The deck's gone! That's what *used* to be here! Now, all we have is this ash. This was the *fourth* fire! We *never* used to have fires like this! Partial burns, yeah, but not these super-hot fire tornadoes that wipe everything out!"

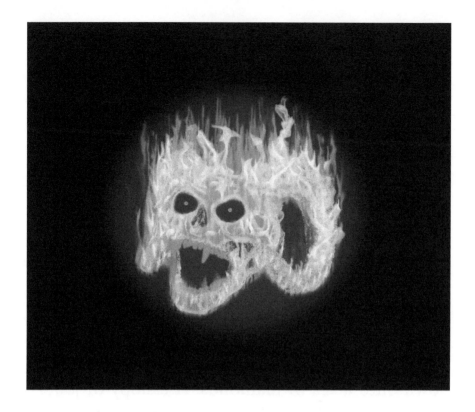

Bailey dropped his head and his voice, then murmured, "And besides, I was busy helping Dad."

"Ah, you were helping your father with the planting. That is good."

She talks weird. And she sure is a long way from home. To her, he said, "But how did you know? About the planting, I mean. Mom and Dad have worked really hard on it. They've put in so many kinds of trees." Bailey stared at what was left of those plantings. Nothing.

"Time is different for me. And that is how I

was able to see the jewels. The tree sea was every green you could know of; green-green, grey-green, blue-green, green of jade, sage, pine, and emerald. Light green, dark green, purple-green, ice-green."

"Ice green?" Bailey queried. "How can you know about so many kinds of green? I mean, where you come from, isn't it all rock and snow and ice and stuff? No trees?"

"Aurora green! Aurora borealis! And did you know, Bailey, borealis means *of the trees*."

"Oh. Sure. I forgot. But I never thought about the borealis part." Despite his awkwardness, he was rewarded by another splendid smile.

"Bailey, I must go home now."

"Home? Where's home, then?"

"My home is the corner of the sky where the stars dance."

He truly did not know how to respond to this.

She continued. "Bailey, I need you to do something. Something very important."

"Um, what do you want me to do?"

"Tell everyone, everyone who has power, that the bears are in the sea." She pointed to the ice block on her sled, which was now almost completely melted.

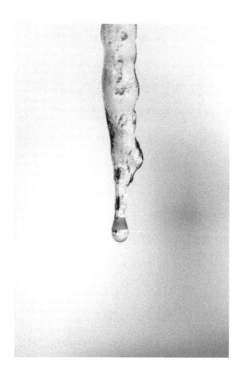

"But who should I tell? What should I do?"

"You don't do anything, Bailey. It is *they* who

must act, once you have told them. They must stop melting the ice."

"You mean climate change. Global warming, don't you." It was a statement, not a question.

"Yes, Bailey."

"But Ursamer, what if they won't do anything? They never do, you know."

"Yes, you are right. They haven't done a thing. They won't listen to facts; I know that now. But maybe, just maybe, they will listen to *magic*."

"Well, I'm pretty sure that's never been tried before! But Ursamer, what if they don't believe me?"

Ursamer gently removed the ice star from Bailey's hand. She shaped it into a collar and put it around Nuga's neck. "Take Nuga with you. He'll convince them."

She gave her dog a fierce hug. It seemed to go on for a very long time, and when she looked up, Bailey saw tears in her eyes.

"Do you have to go? Can't you come with us, Ursamer?"

"No. It is not my place."

Now it was his turn for tears.

"Bailey, Nuga was not engulfed by the sea. He was hurt, but he did not die."

"You mean you're d..."

"Bailey, I am one with the stars now. I am a spirit of light. My family are there. My whole village. But as long as you have this special star, this ice star, you can call me whenever you need me. I promise.

"The ice star has healed Nuga. He should always wear it. But it does have a side effect."

"What's that?"

"Nuga's always real hungry, Bailey! Make sure he gets plenty to eat, won't you."

"Um, sure. Of course I will."

"You and he have hearts of gold. The rest will come. You'll make a great team!"

The dog nuzzled Bailey excitedly. Then yapped for joy.

"Now, here is something else to pass along.

"Nature does not need us. Nature has everything. Beauty, strength, and intelligence. Astounding intelligence! Truly, truly astounding. I'm sure you know that."

The boy was quick to agree. "Yes, Uŕsamer. Every little thing. Every big thing too."

"Bailey, She is the first world. Everything about Her is perfect. Perfect harmony and perfect balance.

"She is superlatively diverse, and it all works.

"Nature has tenacity and resilience, too. Her

healing powers are miraculous, but, only to a point —because of what we have done to her.

"Nature would be much better off without us. But, seeing as we're here, there is something we can do.

"Because there is one thing that Nature does not have. I do not think you will find it in Nature anywhere." Ursamer stopped for a moment, thinking, and then amended, "Although, perhaps some animals come close.

"Bailey, that thing is *compassion*. So, that is what we should give to the equation. Compassion. That is how we fit in to the grand plan. That is our purpose, do you see?"

"Yes, I think so."

Bailey tried not to blush, unsuccessfully. Still, he hung on her every word.

"You possess an abundance of compassion. Use your compassion to save Her, Bailey."

Ursamer hugged her dog and kissed the boy's cheek.

Then, very suddenly, she was gone.

* * *

Sled tracks coursed along the ash bed, and then he could see them climb up into the sky. They were nearly beyond his sight when Uŕsamer turned and waved.

A dried fish spiraled its way downward. The dog barked and jumped to an impossible height, somersaulting in mid-air while securing his treat.

And then they heard, "Bailey! Nuga! Make them understand!"

Dear reader,

We hope you enjoyed reading *Ursamer*. Please take a moment to leave a review, even if it's a short one. Your opinion is important to us.

Discover more books by Karina McRoberts at https://www.nextchapter.pub/authors/karina-mcroberts

Want to know when one of our books is free or discounted? Join the newsletter at http://eepurl.com/bqqB3H

Best regards,
Karina McRoberts and the Next Chapter Team

Escape...

*To the Heights of Your Mind
And the Depths of Your Soul...*

The Real Magic – Courage, Cunning, and Craft trilogy

Galla of Chelandra – Healer Mage

Master of the World – Love and Courage

Juggernaut – Evil and Justice

"Apart from fine adventure, *Galla of Chelandra* will sharpen your admiration for early healers, who faced disaster and disease with great courage." Dr. Duncan Steed, Associate Professor, University of Western Australia Rural School of Medicine

The Love, Magic, and Mystery series

The Palace of the Stars

The Mine's Eye

The Light

"Infectiously fascinating." Grady Harp, 'San Francisco Review of Books'

"Richly realised and highly evocative." William Yeoman, 'The West Australian'

The Treasury of Feel Good Stories series

Dargo, Eco Hero! A Feel-Good Novella

"Can an author of successful mysteries pen an adult fairy tale? The answer is a resounding *YES!*"

Grady Harp, Hall of Fame Top 100 Reviewer

Charlie's Ark, A Feel-Good Nature Story for Children

The Girl With Ten Diamonds, A Feel-Good Novella

The Haunting of York - An Anthology of Ghost Stories

Non-Fiction

Welcome to My Sketchbook - A Beginner's Guide to Creating an Illustrated Travel Journal

Wild at Art! A Beginner's Guide to Drawing and Painting Wildlife

Creative Writing for Beginners - How to Write a Book

Audiobook coming soon!

A Man For All Seasons

(Comedy Fantasy)

ABOUT THE AUTHOR

Karina McRoberts is an Australian scientist, writer, illustrator, musician, and theatre producer.

She lives in historic York, Western Australia's first inland town.

Character research is a favorite past time.

Visit Karina's website:
https://leela5chelandra.wixsite.com/chelandra

Or email her at: leela5chelandra@gmail.com

Or, you can write to her at: P.O. Box 296, York, Western Australia, 6302.

And don't forget the fabulous show, based on
Karina's *Love, Magic, and Mystery* series!
A Night at the Palace of the Stars!
It's the most fun you can have! Go to:
https://www.palaceofthestars.com

Lightning Source UK Ltd.
Milton Keynes UK
UKHW041416091121
393637UK00017B/113